LOVE IN THE TIME OF CHAOS

DIBAKAR BALA

Made with ♥ on the Notion Press Platform
www.notionpress.com

Contents

The Start of a New Beginning

Priya walked down the crowded streets of Mumbai, trying to push her way through the throngs of people. It was just another day in the bustling city, and Priya was already feeling overwhelmed. She was a successful businesswoman, but the constant hustle and bustle of the city always left her feeling drained.

As she made her way to her office building, Priya couldn't help but think about the hook-up culture she had become a part of. She had always been a promiscuous girl, never wanting to settle down with just one man. But lately, she had begun to feel unfulfilled and empty. She craved something more, something real.

She arrived at her office and took a deep breath, trying to push her thoughts aside and focus on work. But even as she sat at her desk and went through her emails, she couldn't shake the feeling that something was missing from her life.

She was so lost in thought that she didn't even hear her coworker, Rohan, approach her. "Hey, Priya," he said, tapping her on the shoulder. She jumped, startled by his sudden presence.

Rohan was a struggling writer who had recently been fired from his job. Despite his setbacks, he had a kind and gentle demeanor that Priya found herself drawn to. She found herself smiling as they struck up a conversation, and for the first time in a long time, she felt genuinely happy.

But little did they know, a deadly virus was sweeping through the city, threatening to destroy everything they held dear. And as the world around them fell into chaos, Priya and Rohan would be forced to fight for their survival and their love.

CHAPTER TWO

Seeking Solace in Each Other

Rohan sat at his desk, staring at the blank page in front of him. He had always dreamed of becoming a successful writer, but lately, it seemed like that dream was slipping further and further away. He had just been fired from his job, and he was struggling to make ends meet.

He sighed and ran his hand through his hair, feeling frustrated and defeated. He was about to give up and call it a day when he heard a knock on his door. He looked up to see Priya standing there, a small smile on her face.

"Hey, Rohan," she said. "Do you have a minute to talk?"

Rohan nodded and gestured for her to come in. Priya took a seat across from him, and for a moment, they sat in silence. Rohan could see the concern in Priya's eyes, and he knew she could sense his struggles.

"I know things have been tough for you lately," Priya said gently. "But I want you to know that you're not alone. I'm here for you, Rohan. And I believe in you."

Rohan felt a surge of emotion at Priya's words. He had always admired her strength and determination, and it meant a lot to him that she was offering him her support.

"Thanks, Priya," he said, his voice choked with emotion. "It means a lot to me that you believe in me. I don't know what I'd do without you."

"You're stronger than you realize, Rohan," Priya said, reaching out to squeeze his hand. "And I have faith that you'll make it through this. We'll make it through this together."

Rohan felt a spark of hope ignite within him, and for the first time in a long time, he felt like he could overcome the challenges ahead. Together, he and Priya would face whatever came their way.

CHAPTER THREE

Falling into Each Other's Arms

Priya felt a mix of emotions as she watched Rohan struggle with his struggles. She cared about him deeply, and she wanted to help him through this difficult time. But she also couldn't deny the attraction she felt towards him.

As she sat across from him, she could feel the sexual tension between them growing. She could see the way his eyes lingered on her, and she knew that he felt it too.

"Rohan," she said softly, leaning in closer to him. "I want to help you. But I also want... more."

Rohan looked at her, his eyes dark with desire. "Priya," he said, his voice low and husky. "I want you too. More than anything."

Priya felt a surge of heat as Rohan reached out to pull her towards him. She wrapped her arms around him, pressing her lips against his in a passionate kiss.

They fell back onto the couch, their bodies entwined as they explored each other's bodies with their hands and lips. Rohan's touch was electric, and Priya could feel herself getting lost in the moment.

"Rohan," she whispered, her breath hot against his ear. "I want you. Right now."

Rohan growled in response, flipping her onto her back and kissing her deeply. They made love right there on the couch, their bodies moving in sync as they gave in to their desire for each other.

Afterwards, they lay tangled in each other's arms, their bodies spent but their hearts full. They had found comfort and solace in each other, and for the first time in a long time, Priya felt truly happy. She knew that whatever challenges lay ahead, she and Rohan would face them together.

CHAPTER FOUR

Realizing True Love

Priya tried to push Rohan out of her mind as she went about her life. She continued to be a successful businesswoman, and she threw herself into her work to try and forget about him. But no matter how hard she tried, she couldn't shake the memories of their time together.

She continued to be a part of the hook-up culture, sleeping with different guys every other day. But as she lay in their arms, she found herself thinking of Rohan. She couldn't help but compare them to him, and she realized that none of them could measure up.

Rohan, on the other hand, couldn't stop thinking about Priya. He tried to reach out to her, but she always seemed to be too busy or too distant. He began to fear that he had lost her forever, and the thought made his heart ache.

But one day, everything changed. Priya received a call from Rohan, and she could hear the desperation in his voice. He begged her to meet him, and she reluctantly agreed.

As she sat across from him, she could see the love and longing in his eyes. And as they talked, she realized that she had been foolish to push him away. She had fallen in love with him, and she knew that she wanted to be with him.

Rohan felt a surge of relief and happiness as Priya admitted her feelings. They embraced, knowing that they had finally found what they had been searching for all along. They vowed to never let each other go, and to face whatever challenges lay ahead together.

CHAPTER FIVE

Facing the Crisis Together

As Rohan and Priya were getting ready to start their new life together, a deadly virus began to sweep through the city of Mumbai. The virus was highly contagious and had a high mortality rate, and it quickly began to spread, causing panic and fear among the population.

The government declared a state of emergency and instituted a lockdown, shutting down all non-essential businesses and ordering people to stay indoors to avoid spreading the virus. Rohan and Priya were forced to put their plans on hold and focus on surviving the outbreak.

They quickly realized that they would need to rely on each other to make it through this crisis. They gathered supplies and stocked up on food and water, knowing that they would need to be self-sufficient in order to survive.

But even as they prepared for the worst, they couldn't help but worry about their loved ones. They knew that many people were falling ill and dying, and they feared for the safety of their friends and families.

As the days passed, the situation continued to deteriorate. The virus showed no signs of slowing down, and the death toll continued to rise. Rohan and Priya did their best to stay safe and healthy, but they knew that they were facing an uncertain future.

They held onto each other, finding comfort and strength in their love. They knew that they would face whatever came their way together, and that their love would be their greatest weapon in the fight against the virus.

CHAPTER SIX

Fighting for a Future Together

As the virus continued to ravage the city, Rohan and Priya faced countless challenges and obstacles. They did their best to stay safe and healthy, but Rohan couldn't help but feel a sense of responsibility to help others.

Despite Priya's protests, Rohan began to venture out into the city to help those in need. He distributed supplies to those who were struggling and did whatever he could to provide assistance.

Priya was terrified for Rohan's safety, and she begged him to stop. But he was determined to do what he could to help, and he refused to listen to her.

As the days passed, Rohan became increasingly selfless and focused on helping others. He put his own safety aside, and he risked his life to save others.

Despite their best efforts, Rohan and Priya were eventually forced to flee the city and seek refuge in a remote location. They managed to make it through the crisis, but Rohan's health had been severely compromised by the virus.

Priya did everything she could to help him, and she was relieved when he began to show signs of improvement.

Slowly but surely, Rohan regained his strength, and he was able to recover from the virus.

They were both deeply grateful to have made it through the crisis, and they vowed to never take their love for granted again. They knew that they would face whatever challenges came their way together, and that their love would be their greatest weapon in the fight for a better future.

CHAPTER SEVEN

Finding Strength in Love and Memory

Priya was overjoyed when she learned that Rohan was recovering from the virus. She had been terrified of losing him, and she was grateful that he was getting better.

But as the days passed, Priya began to notice that Rohan wasn't quite himself. He seemed distant and preoccupied, and he was hiding something from her.

One day, she found a folder in Rohan's bag that contained the results of his latest medical tests. She was shocked and devastated to see that the virus had done serious damage to his body, and that he didn't have long to live.

Rohan had kept the truth from her to spare her from the pain and heartache. He wanted her to remember him as he was, not as the sick and dying man he had become.

Priya was devastated when she learned the truth, but she was also grateful for the time they had together. She decided to make the most of their remaining time, and to cherish every moment they had left.

She and Rohan spent their days together, talking, laughing, and making memories. And at night, they gave in to their passion and desire for each other.

"Rohan," Priya whispered, her breath hot against his ear. "I want you. Right now."

Rohan growled in response, flipping her onto her back and kissing her deeply. They made love with a sense of urgency and intensity, knowing that it could be their last time together.

In the end, they were able to find happiness and peace in each other's arms.

And as Rohan took his last breath, Priya knew that she would never forget him. She was heartbroken and devastated by his loss, but she also knew that their love had been strong enough to overcome even the greatest of challenges.

She took comfort in the memories of their time together, and she vowed to never forget the power of love in the face of chaos. She would honor Rohan's memory by continuing to fight for a better future, and by never giving up hope.

As she mourned his loss, Priya also found strength in the knowledge that she had been lucky enough to experience true love. She had been able to find happiness and fulfillment in her relationship with Rohan, and that was something that no one could take away from her.

And so, Priya continued on, determined to make the most of her life and to never forget the lessons she had learned from Rohan. She knew that she would always carry him with her, and that their love would continue to inspire her long after he was gone.

CHAPTER EIGHT

Honoring the Legacy of Love

Years have passed since Rohan's death, and Priya has made a new life for herself. She has continued to be successful in her career, and she has used her wealth and influence to start a non-profit organization in Rohan's name. The organization provides support and assistance to those affected by the virus outbreak, and it is a testament to Rohan's selflessness and bravery.

Priya is no longer the promiscuous girl she once was. She has learned the value of love and commitment, and she has dedicated herself to helping others. She is a loving mother to her daughter, who was born from Rohan, and she is grateful for the time she had with him.

Though Rohan was a struggling writer and not particularly successful, he left a lasting impact on Priya. He taught her the power of love and the importance of compassion, and he helped her to become a better person. She will always carry him with her, and she will never forget the lessons he taught her.

As she looks to the future, Priya is determined to continue fighting for a better world. She knows that she can never bring Rohan back, but she can honor his memory by making the most of her life and by helping others. She is grateful for the love they shared, and she knows that their love will continue to inspire and guide her for the rest of her days.

• 16 •